CAPTAIN AWESOME

and the MUMMY'S TREASURE

By STAN KIRBY

Illustrated by GEORGE O'CONNOR

LITTLE SIMON

New York   London   Toronto   Sydney   New Delhi

LITTLE SIMON

An imprint of Simon & Schuster Children's Publishing Division • 1230 Avenue of the Americas, New York, New York 10020 • First Little Simon hardcover edition November 2015. Copyright © 2015 by Simon & Schuster, Inc. All rights reserved, including the right of reproduction in whole or in part in any form. LITTLE SIMON is a registered trademark of Simon & Schuster, Inc., and associated colophon is a trademark of Simon & Schuster, Inc. For information about special discounts for bulk purchases, please contact Simon & Schuster Special Sales at 1-866-506-1949 or business@simonandschuster.com. The Simon & Schuster Speakers Bureau can bring authors to your live event. For more information or to book an event contact the Simon & Schuster Speakers Bureau at 1-866-248-3049 or visit our website at www.simonspeakers.com. Designed by Jay Colvin. The text of this book was set in Little Simon Gazette.

Manufactured in the United States of America 1015 FFG

10 9 8 7 6 5 4 3 2 1

Cataloguing-in-Publication Data for this title is available from the Library of Congress.

ISBN 978-1-4814-4439-2 (hc)

ISBN 978-1-4814-4438-5 (pbk)

ISBN 978-1-4814-4440-8 (eBook)

Table of Contents

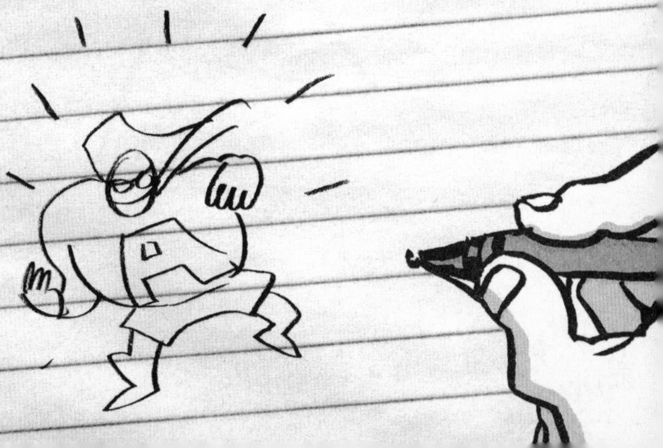

CHAPTER I

Field Trip of Mystery

By
Eugene

Beware the pencil power of of the Power Pencil,' says evil Lord Stickman!" Eugene McGillicudy whispered. He scribbled his pencil across his notebook where he had drawn a stick figure villain wearing a crown and holding a laser.

"What do you think, Eugene?" His best friend, Charlie Thomas Jones, held up his own drawing. It was a pile of liquid yellow

cheese with red and blue spots. "Stick Figure Nacho Cheese Man just covered Stick Figure King Boulderface in hot pepper cheese," Charlie said. "I colored the cheese."

"What's with the blue spots?"

"My red marker dried out,"

Charlie explained. "So, who's going to defeat Lord Stickman?"

"Why, the only one who can." Eugene quickly drew a stick figure man with a cape and giant hands. "Super Dude."

BAM!

"And the town of Dudeville cheered for their hero, the greatest superhero ever!" Eugene said.

What's that you say?! You've never heard of Super Dude? Do you live in a cave and eat nothing but moldy fruit strips?

Super Dude is the superhero who once scored an A-Plus Punch on the Question Marker's Quiz of Destruction.

Super Dude is the star of his own comic books, cartoon shows, movies, video games, *and* theme park. He's also the reason that Eugene, Charlie, and their other friend Sally Williams became Sunnyview's own superheroes!

CLAP-CLAP! CLAP!

Eugene jumped in his seat. His pencil accidentally scratched across the page like a lightning bolt. But the clapping sound wasn't Captain Lightning McThunderclap or the Claptomaniak attacking Sunnyview. Their teacher, Ms. Beasley, was clapping her hands to get everyone's attention.

"Class, I have exciting news," she said. "Tomorrow, we're going on a surprise field trip!"

**GASP!
CHEER!**

"Field trips are better than extra dessert at lunch!" Eugene whispered to Charlie.

WHERE? WHERE? WHERE?

Everyone in the class was asking the same question.

Sally raised her hand. "How fast can we get there?"

"See if you can solve this riddle,"

Ms. Beasley said. "It's a very cool place filled with very old things, where monsters sit beside ancient kings."

"Oh! It's Cheese King Land!" Charlie yelled out. "And we're going to eat Royal Burgers and Lord of the Fries!"

Sally leaned over to Charlie. "There's no Cheese King Land in Sunnyview."

"A kid can dream," Charlie replied dreamily.

At recess the only thing everyone was talking about was:

Who would solve Ms. Beasley's riddle first?

"I think it's Pink Palace Park," said Meredith Mooney, the pinkest girl in school. If there was a dress made of pink puke, she'd wear it. Today the pink ribbon in her hair matched her pink shoelaces and her pink bracelets.

"I think we're going to Cowboy Village," said Gil Ditko.

"Or the Sunnyview Speedway!" said Marlo Craven.

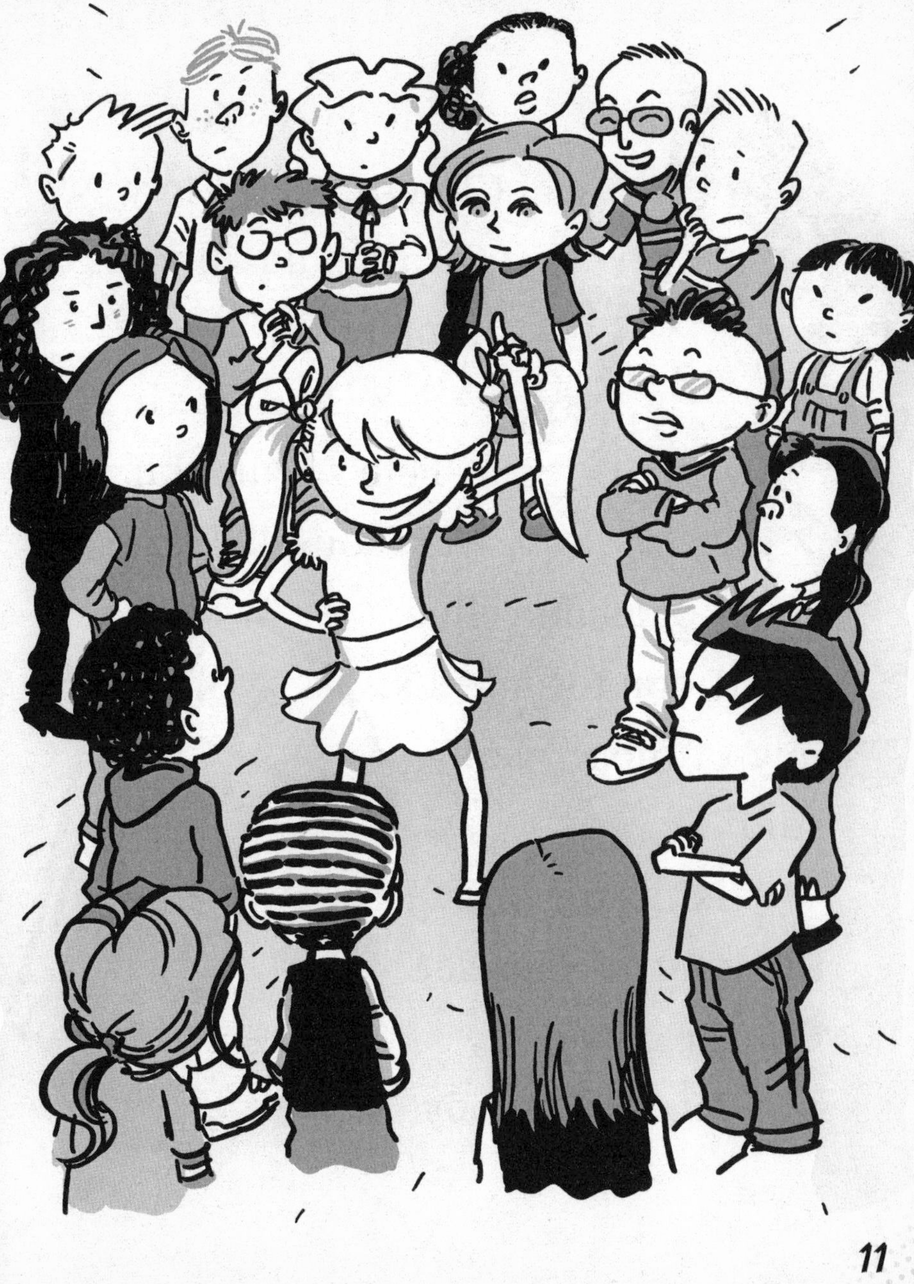

"Calamity Kate's Clam-tastic Clam Farm!" said Olivia Simonson.

"Pumpkin Pete's Pumpkin Warehouse!" Evan Mason yelled.

"I don't think it's any of those," Sally said.

"Isn't anyone thinking of cheese?" Charlie asked.

Before anybody

could agree on the riddle's answer, the bell rang. Recess was over. The class ran back in to try their guesses on Ms. Beasley.

"The Sunnyview Superhero Squad will have to solve this riddle!" Eugene pointed in the direction of his home. "To the clubhouse! MI-TEE!"

"CHEESY YO!" yelled Charlie.

"SPEEDY GO!" shouted Sally.

Eugene started to run.

"Wait. Eugene!" Sally called out. "School's not done yet!"

OOPS!

"Oh . . . right. Okay, we'll meet after school and solve this riddle!" Eugene said. "Because that's what heroes do!"

CHAPTER 2

Guessing Game

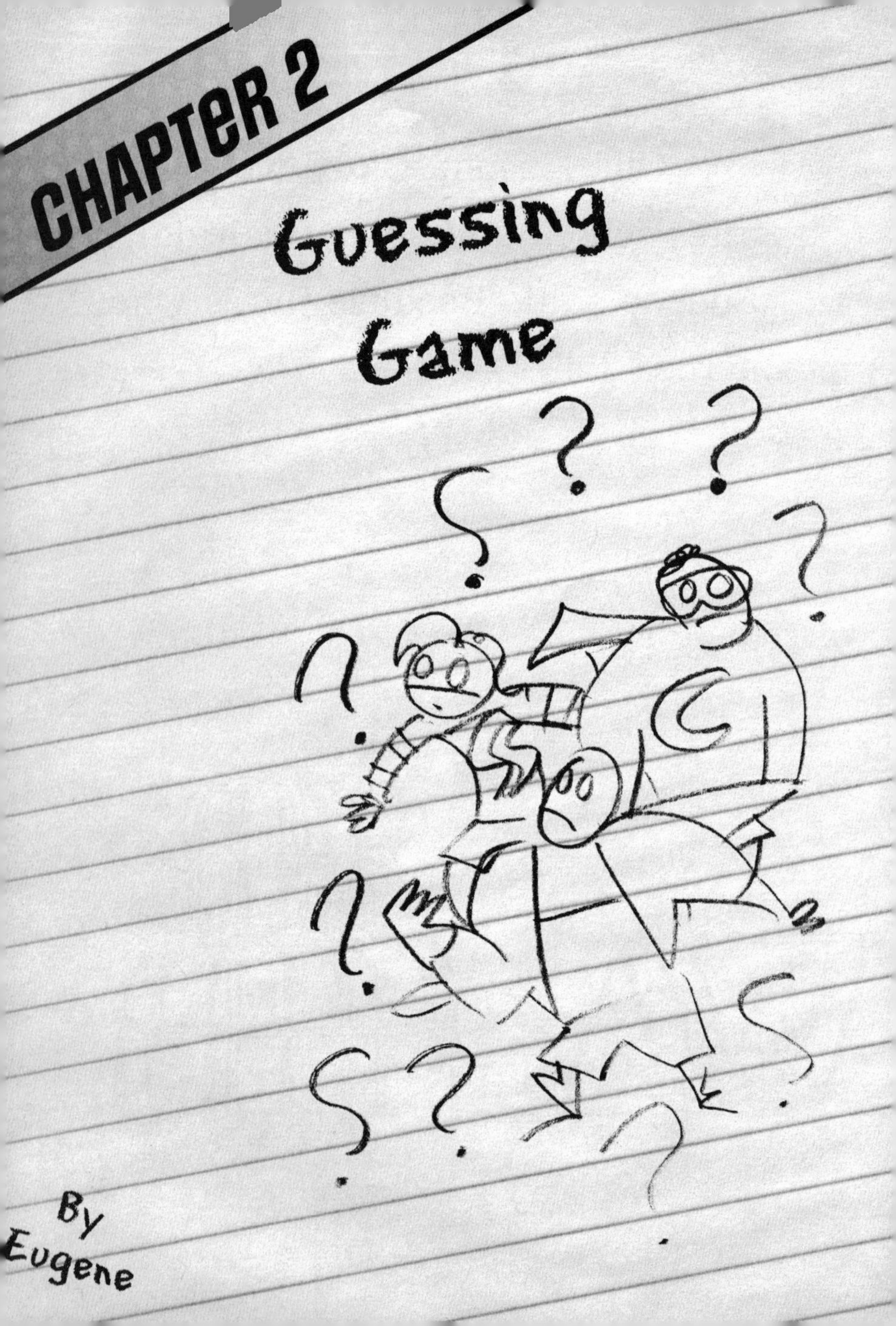

By Eugene

By three o'clock, the Sunnyview Superhero Squad was in their secret headquarters in a tree in the McGillicudys' backyard. Captain Awesome, Nacho Cheese Man, and Supersonic Sal were dressed and ready for riddle-solving action.

"The Board of Answers shall reveal all!" Supersonic Sal said as she finished writing the clues on a whiteboard nailed to the wall.

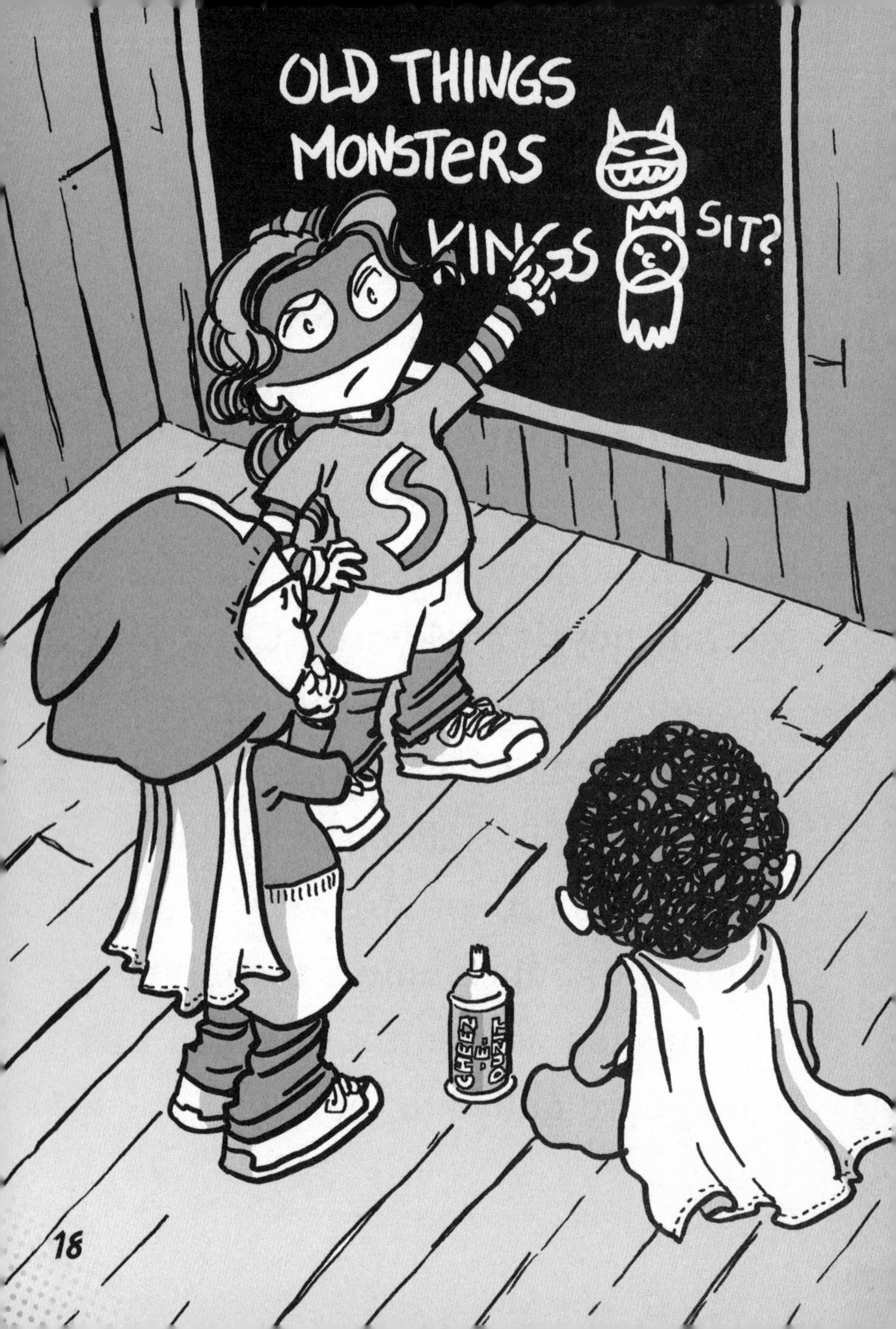
OLD THINGS
MONSTERS
KINGS
SIT?
CHEEZ-E-DUZIT

Captain Awesome read the riddle again. "It's a very cool place filled with very old things, where monsters sit beside ancient kings."

Nacho Cheese Man leaped to his feet. "The Sunnyview Comic Book Mines at the edge of town!"

"There's no comic book mine in Sunnyview," Supersonic Sal said.

"That's the surprise!" Nacho Cheese Man said.

Supersonic Sal rolled her eyes. "It's not comic books."

"What do you think it is then?" Nacho Cheese Man asked.

"It might be the zoo," Supersonic Sal said.

"I love the zoo!" Captain Awesome said.

"I know, right?" Supersonic Sal said. "Lions are the king of the jungle and some of those turtles are really old and those snakes . . . yikes!" Supersonic Sal shivered. "Just like monsters!"

Nacho Cheese Man folded his  across his chest. "It can't be the zoo. It's cool but we were just there."

Captain Awesome agreed. "That's the only bad thing about great field trips—no repeats!"

Captain Awesome ran the clues through his brain. What would Super Dude do to figure it out? Of course, he'd program the equation into his Super Dude tablet and have

the answer before snack time.

Cool place.

Very old things.

Sitting beside kings.

Sunnyview had no kings, so this guy must be from out of town. Or maybe "king" means something big, like king-size. Old things might be dead things, or something really old like the table in the dining room, or something not as old like a rare comic book. And where's a place to buy cool, old, king-size comics?

OF COURSE!

"I've got it!" Captain Awesome snapped his fingers.

"Is it the mine?" Nacho Cheese Man asked.

"There's no mine," Super-sonic Sal said.

"It's not a mine," said Captain Awe-some. "Or a zoo.  It's a place that sells old things that are king-size."

"Eugene!" Captain Awesome's mom called out from the kitchen

window. "Time for dinner and then bed! You need a good night's sleep for your field trip to Sunnyview's museum."

"A MUSEUM?!" the Sunnyview Superhero Squad said at the same time.

"Yes. Of course. A museum. Ha-ha!" Captain Awesome said. "That's totally what I was going to say. Museum. *So* obvious . . ."

The trio climbed down the ladder. As the friends disappeared into

the dark backyard, Nacho Cheese
Man said hopefully, "Maybe it's a
comic book museum. . . ."

CHAPTER 3

Everything Is So Old!

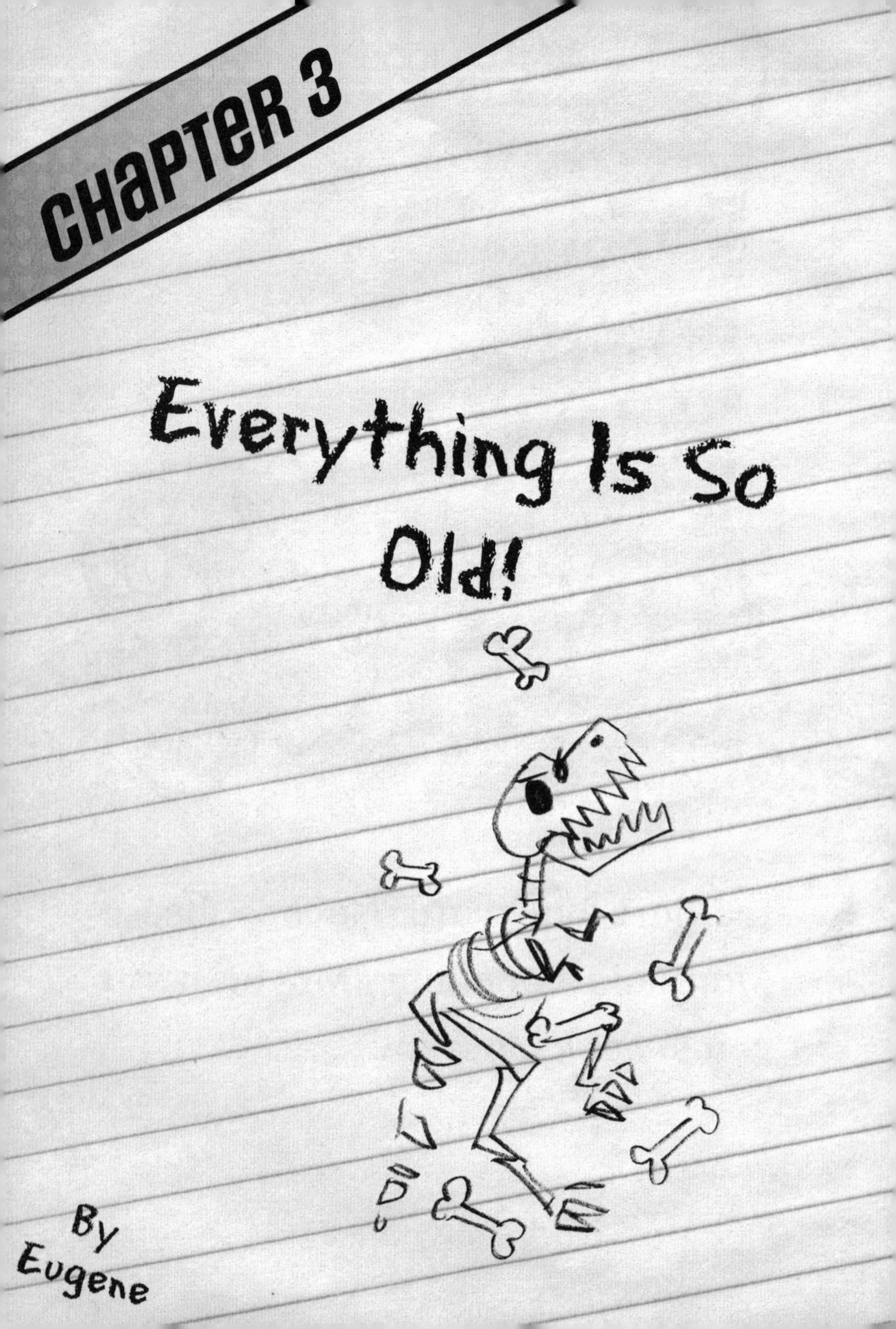

By Eugene

YEAH!

A Tyrannosaurus rex skeleton stood in the lobby of the Sunnyview Art and History Museum. Its bony jaws were ready to snap if any kid got too close.

WOW!
AWESOME!

"Dinosaur bones are awesome!" Eugene exclaimed.

"You guys are such dorks,"

Meredith said. She walked past them wearing a bright pink hat and matching pink gloves. "This is a museum of art and history. It's

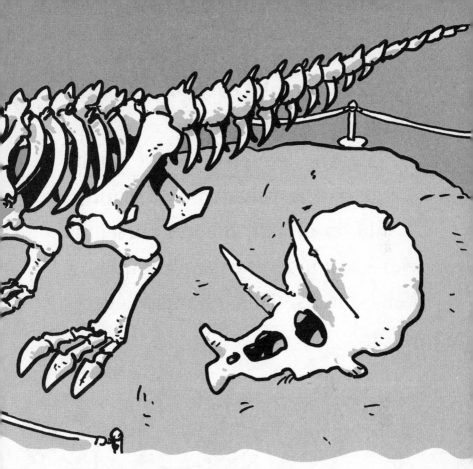

full of bones. Geez. What were you
expecting?"

"But T. rex bones are so cool!"
Charlie protested.

"They might even be the best thing ever!" Sally agreed.

Eugene leaned as close to the T. rex as the velvet rope around it would let him. "I thought museums were nothing but cobwebs and broken statues. This changes everything."

"Come along, class! Line up," Ms. Beasley said. "We can't stare at the dinosaur all day. There's plenty more to see!"

The students lined up behind a big security guard. He wore a dark blue uniform with a silver badge

over one pocket. He had a flashlight in his right hand.

"Single file, children," said
the security guard. "Single. File."
His voice sounded like a wash-
ing machine filled
with sandpaper and
rocks. "No gum-
chewing allowed,
no spitting, no
sticky sodas, and
no spitting gum and soda. This is a
museum, not a movie theater . . . or
a comic book store."

Eugene elbowed Charlie.

"Ow!" Charlie said. "What's that for?"

"That's no ordinary security guard," Eugene said.

Sally nodded.

"Who is it?" Charlie asked.

"I don't know," Eugene said. "But we'll have to keep an eye on him."

"Good thing we brought our superhero suits," Sally whispered.

"And I brought an extra-large can of cheese!" added Charlie.

The trio passed the security guard and joined the other kids in line. Eugene patted his backpack. His Captain Awesome suit was inside.

WHISTLE!

The kids stood still. A tall blond woman wearing an explorer's hat, a tan explorer's outfit, and a large gold whistle stood in front of the class.

"I'm Maggie Van Winkel. Welcome to the Sunnyview Art and History Museum. I'll be your guide today." Her voice echoed through the museum. She pointed to the T. rex skeleton behind them. "I see you met George. He's from Wyoming! Now, follow me . . . for the adventure of a lifetime!"

She led the kids from the lobby through a large archway. Her arms waved excitedly as she talked.

"Today you'll see so many things!" she said. "George is one of our monsters. Now we'll go see an ancient king. Or two. And who knows? We might even find some . . . treasure!"

Eugene, Charlie, and Sally looked at one another.

TREASURE?!

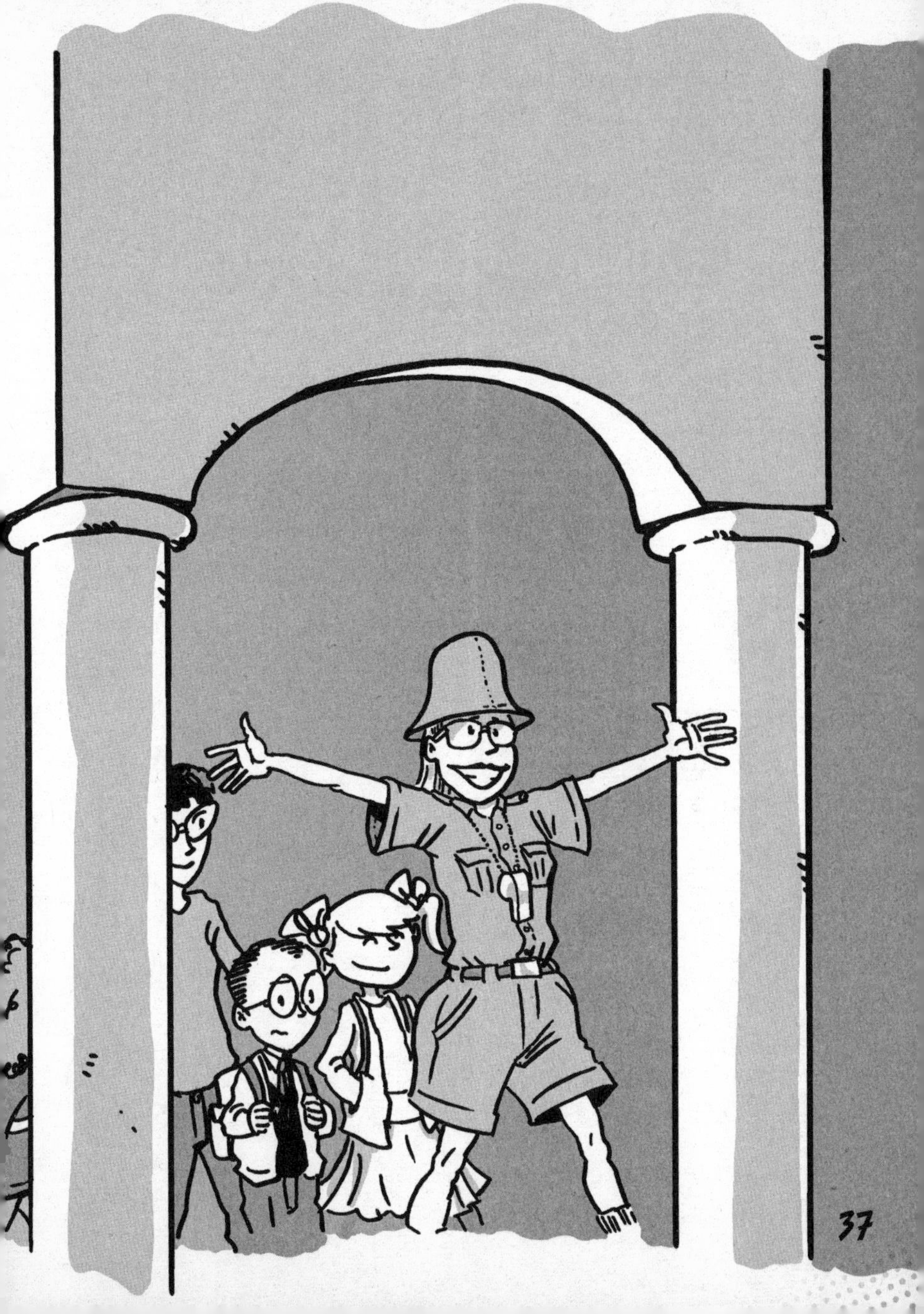

CHAPTER 4

The Treasure Hunters

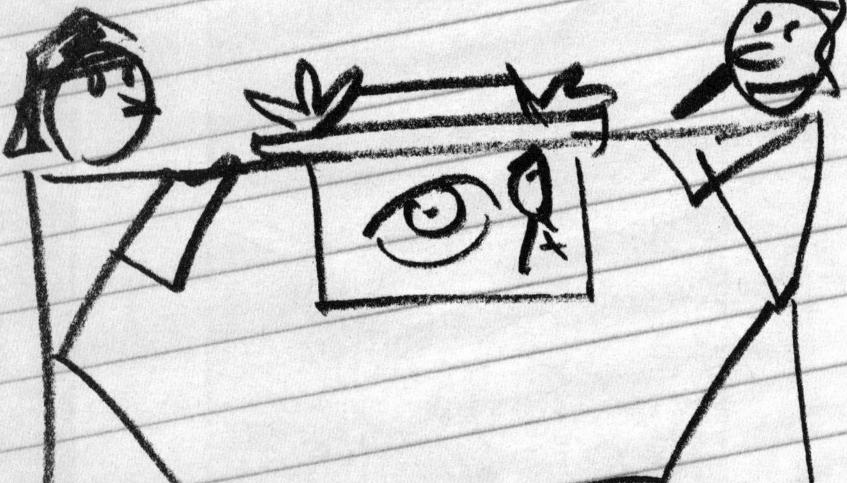

By
Eugene

The class walked into a room that looked like it was carved out of rock. In it was a pyramid surrounded by statues, and rows of glass cases filled with bits of stone, iron, and pots.

"Welcome to ancient Egypt!" Ms. Van Winkel said. "The items here are thousands of years old."

"Thousands?" Sally repeated. "Wow!"

"That's older than my dad," Charlie said.

"And what do you think's inside the pyramid?" Ms. Van Winkel asked the class.

"Smaller pyramids," shouted Olivia.

"Sand!" cried Wilma. "I'm already itchy."

"A weather machine created by evil Count Pharaoh to destroy the world!" Eugene said.

"No, it's not another pyramid, or sand, or

what you said about destroying the world," said the guide. "Inside are . . . mummies!"

WHOA!
MUMMIES!

"Bring on the monsters!" Charlie yelled.

"Mummies aren't monsters," Ms. Van Winkel said. "They're ancient kings, and the pyramids are where they were buried when they died. They took all of their gold and jewels along with them."

GOLD . . .
JEWELS . . .
TREASURE!

"Did you hear what she said?"

Charlie whispered.

"There's a mummy's treasure here!" Sally clapped her hands together.

Meanwhile, Eugene stood in front of a glass display case against the wall. Inside were two stone rectangles. Tiny pictures were carved into the stone. The pictures showed

ancient Egyptians walking, run-
ning, playing games, carrying food,
and more.

"It looks like a picture book,"
Sally said, coming over.

"Better." Eugene smiled. "This
could be the first comic book ever."

"Maybe this *is* a comic book mine after all!" Charlie said.

Eugene pointed to the first row of pictures in the stone. "Look, this guy might be the king. He has the biggest hat."

"What are these guys doing over here?" Charlie pointed to the image of men carrying a large chest over to a hole in the ground.

"Looks like they're burying something," Sally replied.

"And there's writing on the vase next to them," Eugene remarked.

"What's the vase doing there?" Charlie asked.

CLUE!

"I'll bet it's telling us where the treasure's buried!" Sally cried.

"If we find the treasure, the Sunnyview Superhero Squad

will be mummy museum heroes!"
Eugene said excitedly.

"And with the reward, we can
get new stuff for the clubhouse,"
Charlie added.

"Maybe a new crime computer," Sally chimed.

"A meeting table!" said Charlie.

"You're forgetting the one thing all kids need," Eugene pointed out.

"A never-ending supply of Super Dude comic books!" the three friends said at once.

Sally took out a notepad from her backpack. "I'll write down the clues so we can follow them to the treasure." She began quickly scribbling.

Eugene looked around the room. "If we find it before anyone else, this will be the best field trip ever," he said.

Charlie said it first. "To the costumes!"

BACKPACKS!
UNZIP!
CAPE!
SUPERHEROES!

"Let's follow
the clues,"
Captain
Awesome
said.

"Where do we
start?" Nacho
Cheese Man
asked.

Supersonic Sal pointed to the exit. Next to it was a statue with a dog's head that was facing toward another room. "I think he's pointing the way."

"An ancient dog would never lie," Captain Awesome said confidently.

The Sunnyview Superhero Squad snuck away from their class and entered the next room.

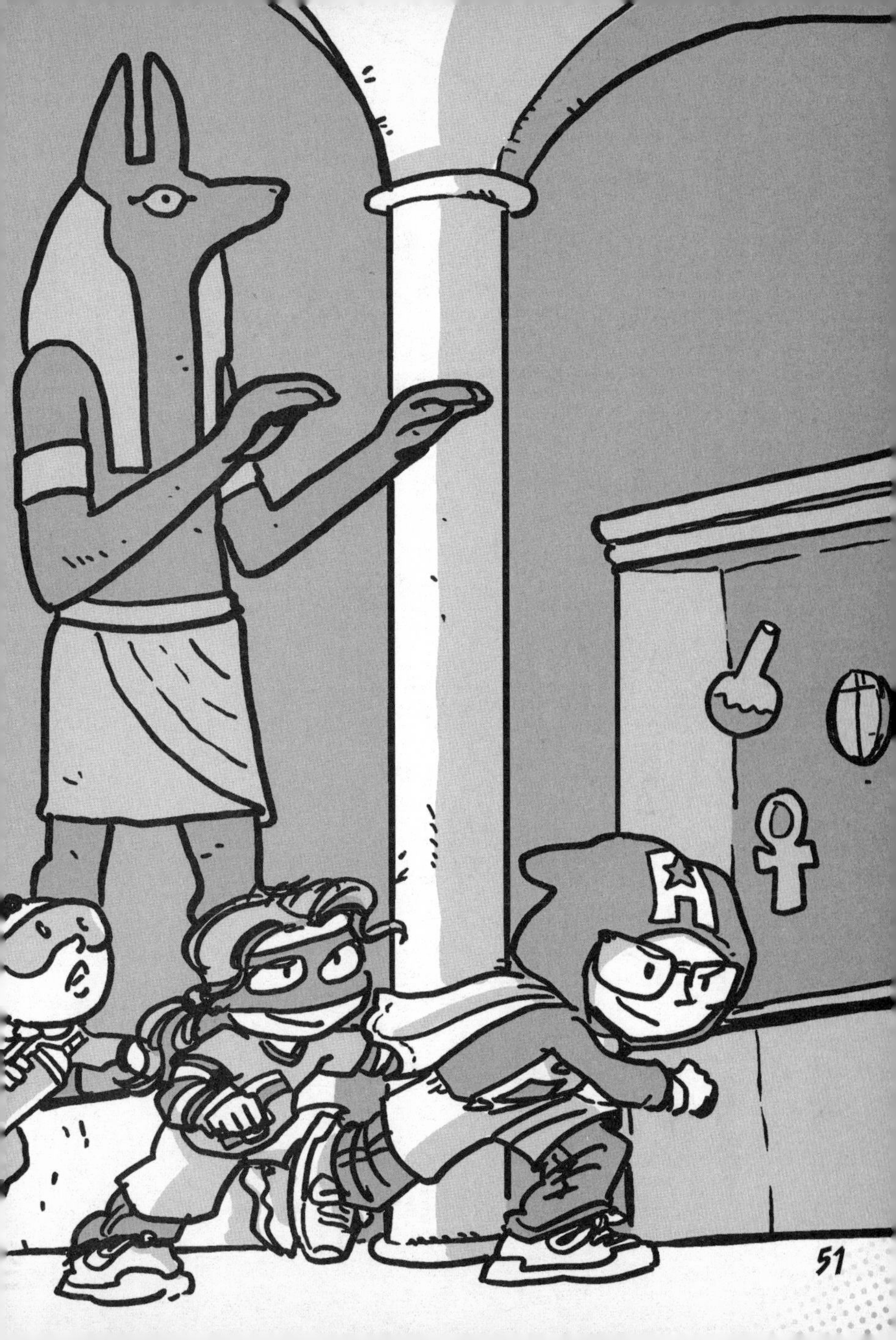

CHAPTER 5

It's All Greek to Me

BY
Eugene

"This must be ancient Greece,"
Supersonic Sal said.

"Look at all the snow sculp-
tures!" Nacho Cheese Man said.

"That's marble," said Captain
Awesome. "The ancient Greeks
made lots of stuff out of marble.
Even toilets."

"But not the toilet paper, right?"
Nacho Cheese Man asked.

Marble statues stood on

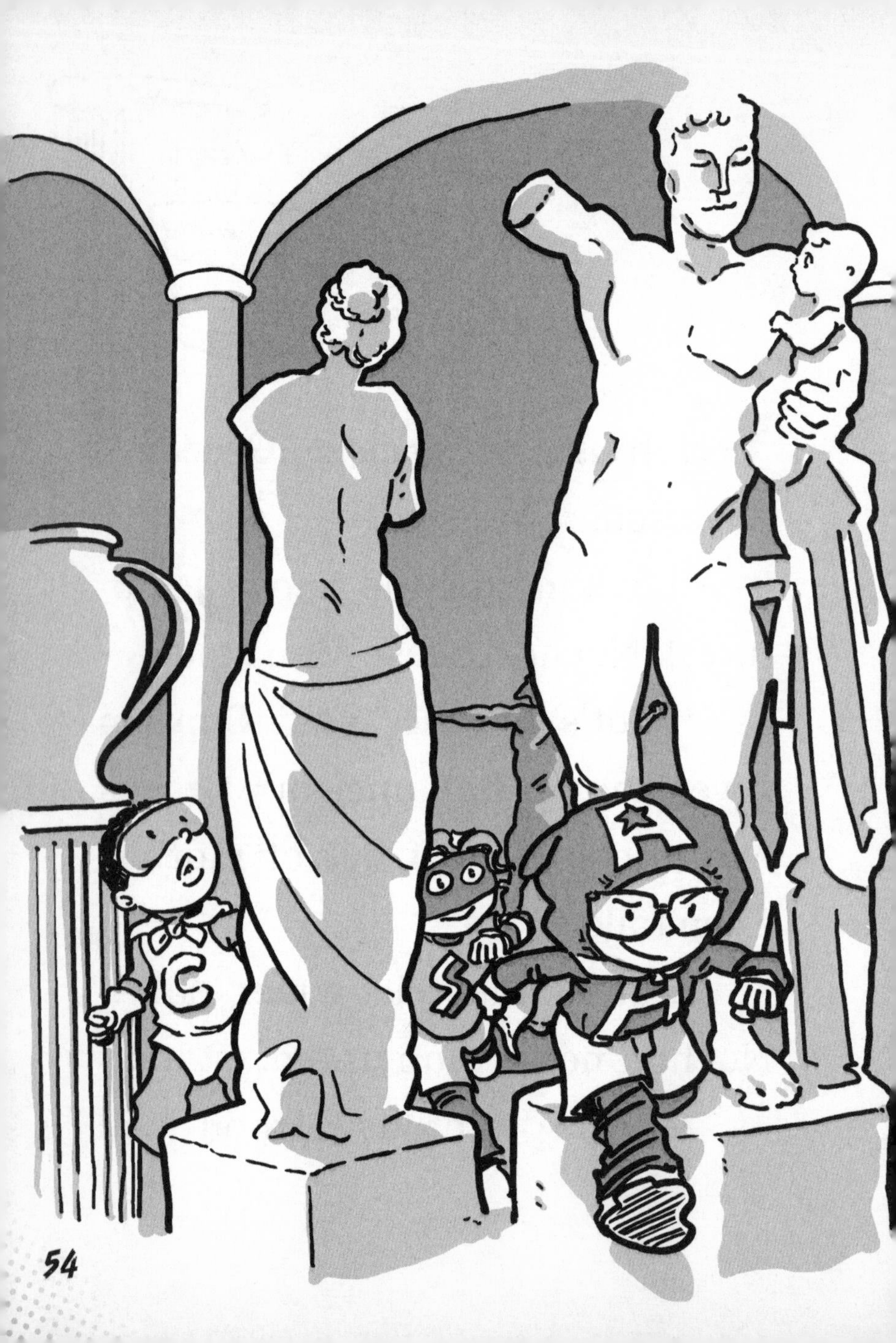

pedestals around the room. They were smooth and white as . . . snow. Some of them were missing an arm or a leg or a nose. Some held swords, spears, and shields.

The heroes walked between the statues, on the lookout for any clues.

Nacho Cheese Man stopped next to a large white vase. "Look at this crazy flower pot . . . oops!"

OOPS?!

Nacho Cheese Man had accidentally bumped into the stand. The vase started to wobble.

SPIN!
TEETER!
TOTTER!

Supersonic Sal dove in front of Nacho Cheese Man like a bolt of lightning. She grabbed the stand with both hands and held it until the wobbling stopped. The vase was saved!

"Great job, Sal!"

Captain Awesome said. "There could be more booby traps here."

"So what are we looking for?" Nacho Cheese Man asked. "Are there any clues in ancient Greece?"

Supersonic Sal glanced down at her notebook. One of the pictures had

shown an Egyptian woman balancing a *vase* on her head.

CLUE!

They all slowly turned to the booby-trapped vase that had attacked Nacho Cheese Man.

"Way to go, Sal!" Nacho Cheese Man said.

"If we just keep on following the clues, we'll find the treasure," Captain Awesome said.

Supersonic Sal looked at her notebook. "The next clue is a snake."

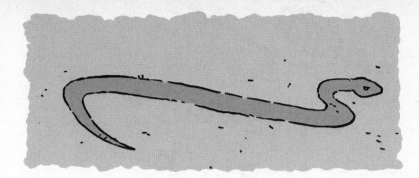

"At this rate, we'll have this mystery solved before lunch," Captain Awesome said.

RUMBLE!

Nacho Cheese Man pointed to his stomach. "I'm already hungry."

But Captain Awesome was heading toward the next room. Supersonic Sal and Nacho Cheese Man ran to keep up with him.

CHAPTER 6

Drawing a Blank

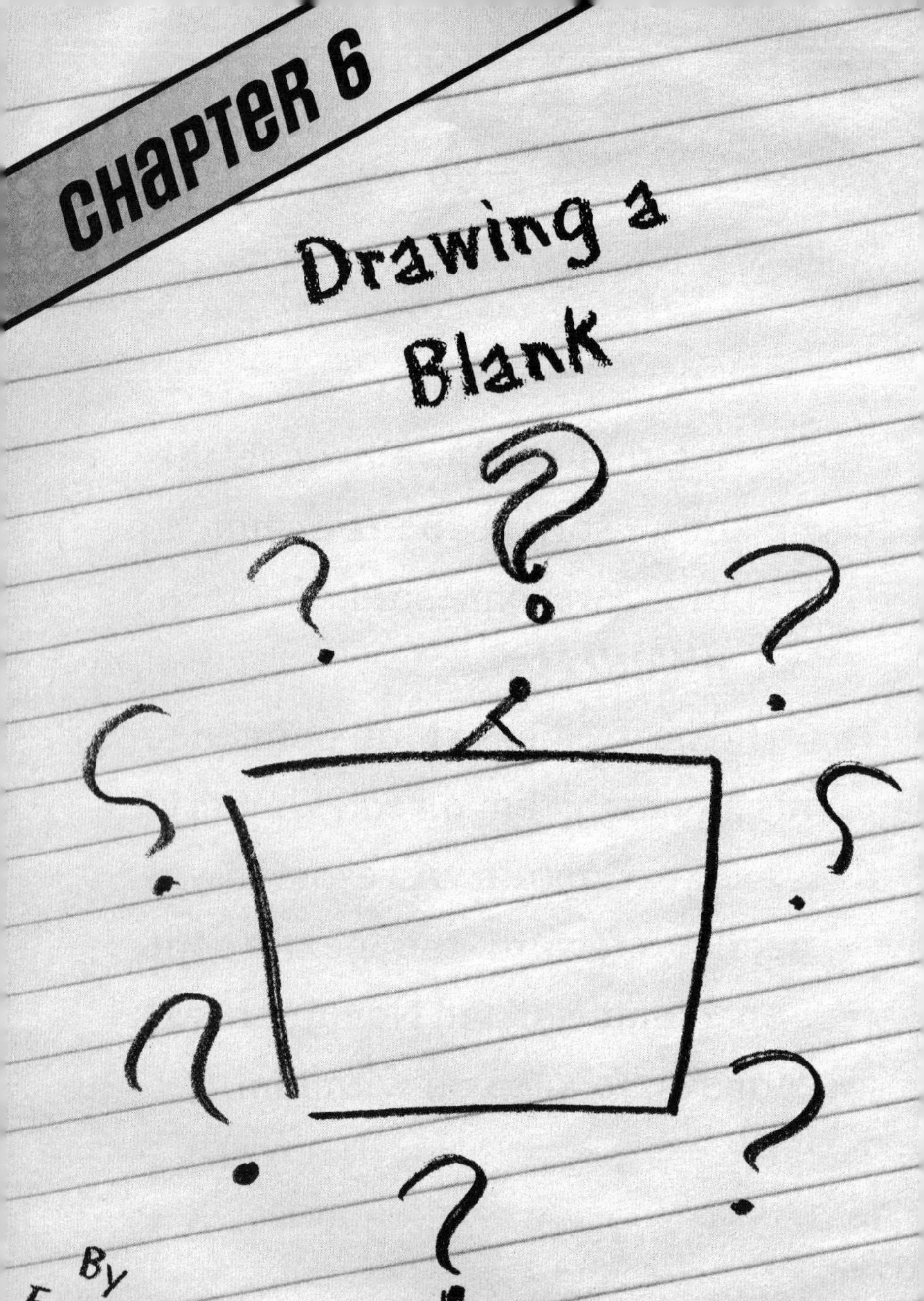

By Eugene

Whoooooaaaaa . . . ," the
trio of do-gooders said in unison
as they crept into the medieval
wing of the museum.

Before them were swords,
flags with cool coats of arms, a
huge model of a castle, and best
of all . . .

"Knights!" Captain Awesome
gasped. "They were superheroes of
medieval times . . . except without

cool costumes or superpowers. This
museum is getting more awesome
with each room. . . ."

"Remember when Super Dude
went back in time to battle the
wicked Sir Lance-a-Lotta-Pasta

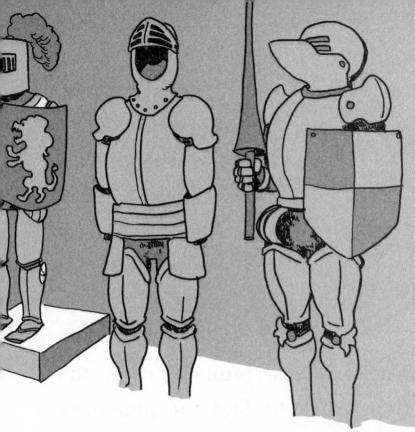

and his evil Knight-mare Knights of the Square Table in Super Dude number five hundred?!" Supersonic Sal asked, admiring an all-black suit of armor.

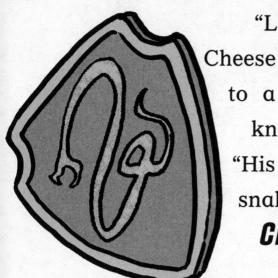

"Look!" Nacho Cheese Man pointed to a shield in a knight's hand. "His shield has a snake on it!"

CLUE!

"Good job, Nacho Cheese Man! We're on the right track to find the mummy's treasure," Captain Awesome said.

Supersonic Sal checked the next drawing in her notebook. "Now we need to find a boat."

With Supersonic Sal leading

the way, the three heroes crept into the art gallery. Dozens of paintings hung from the walls. Nacho Cheese Man stopped in front of a huge, totally blank canvas.

"This one speaks to me," he said, squirting a dollop of cheese onto his tongue.

"Is it saying, 'Help! A supervillain stole all the paint off me?!'" Captain Awesome asked with a chuckle.

"No one stole the paint. It's *supposed* to look like that," Supersonic Sal said.

"Really?" Captain Awesome said in disbelief. "It's blank."

Captain Awesome dug into his utility pocket, which was filled

with random super items that he
might need in the case of a super
emergency: string, a stick of gum,
a button, and a folded-up piece of
paper. He unfolded the paper to
reveal a drawing of Super Dude
he had secretly made in school.

He chewed up a small piece of the gum, attached it to the back of his drawing, and stuck it on an empty space on the wall.

"Now *that's* art!" he said.

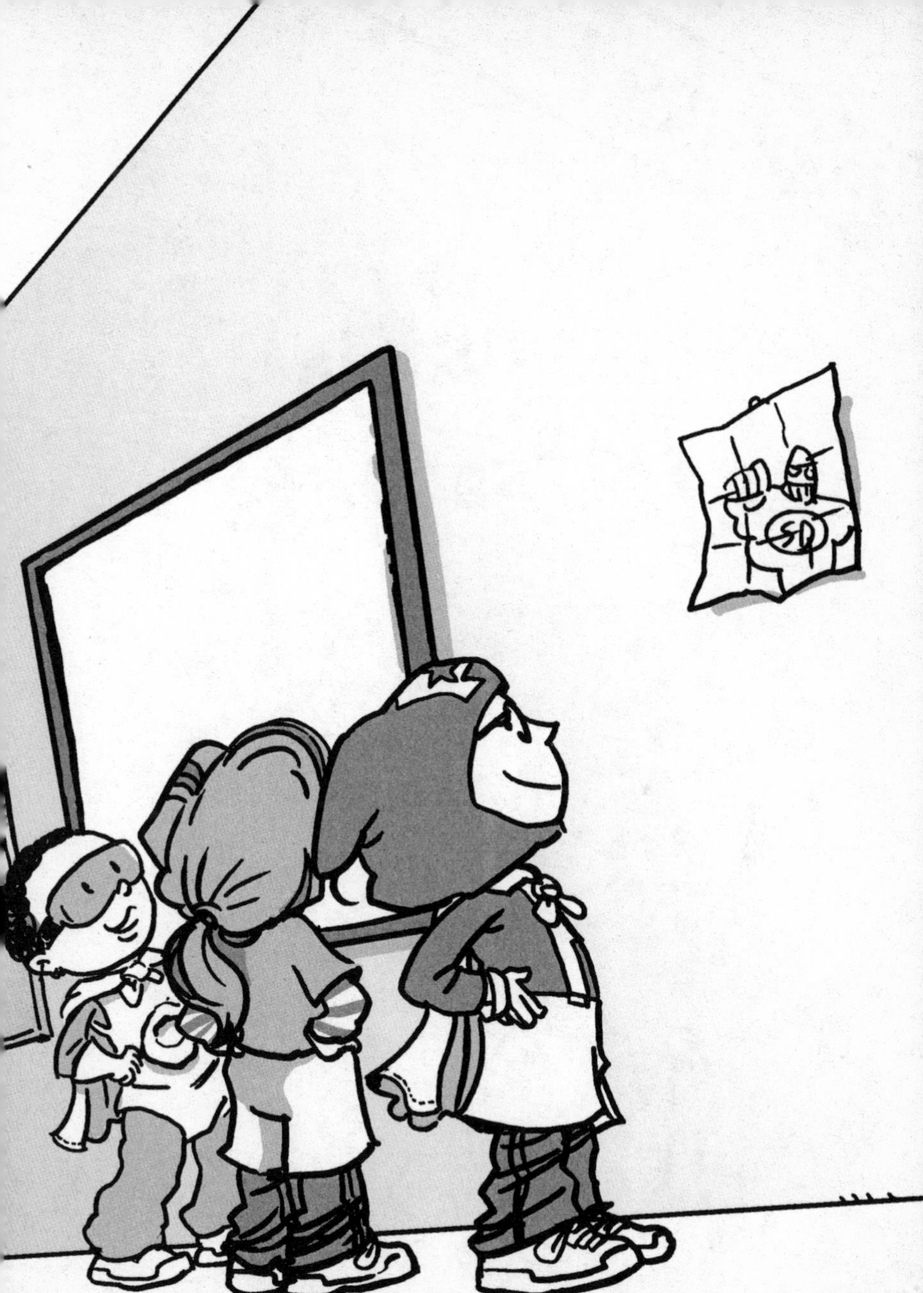

CHAPTER 7

Lost in Lotsa Dots

By
Eugene

With the art gallery made even more awesome by Captain Awesome's awesome drawing of awesomeness, the heroes passed one final painting, which was even bigger than the blank canvas.

"Oh, check it out," Captain Awesome said. "The whole painting is made of, like, a jillion dots."

"It says it was painted by some guy named, uh, it says, uh, 'Sewer

Rat,'" Nacho Cheese Man stammered as he tried to read the name.

"His name is S-e-u-r-a-t. It's pronounced 'Sir-ah,'" Supersonic Sal said, correcting him. "We learned

about him in art class. Remember?"

"I like Sewer Rat." Nacho Cheese Man pulled out his canned cheese but it slipped from his fingers and rolled across the floor.

He raced after his runaway
cheese can, and when he turned
around, he saw
something
amazing.
"Guys!
I found the
boat!" he
called out.

"Where?!" asked a confused Captain Awesome, looking around.

"You're standing right in front of it!" Nacho Cheese Man pointed at the painting across the room. "Look!"

Captain Awesome scanned the dots in the Seurat painting. "You see any boat?" he asked Sal.

"I see dots. Lots and lots and *lots* of dots," Supersonic Sal replied.

"I think you're full of canned cheese," Captain Awesome called out to Nacho Cheese Man.

"No! Come here! You can't see it close up," Nacho Cheese Man grabbed Captain Awesome and Supersonic Sal and led them to the other side of the room.

"Mi-tee . . ." Captain Awesome said the moment he turned to look at the Seurat painting.

CLUE!

It may have *looked* like a mess of dots when they were standing close to the painting, but when they looked at it from across the room, the dots formed a picture of a boat!

"This guy must've painted it

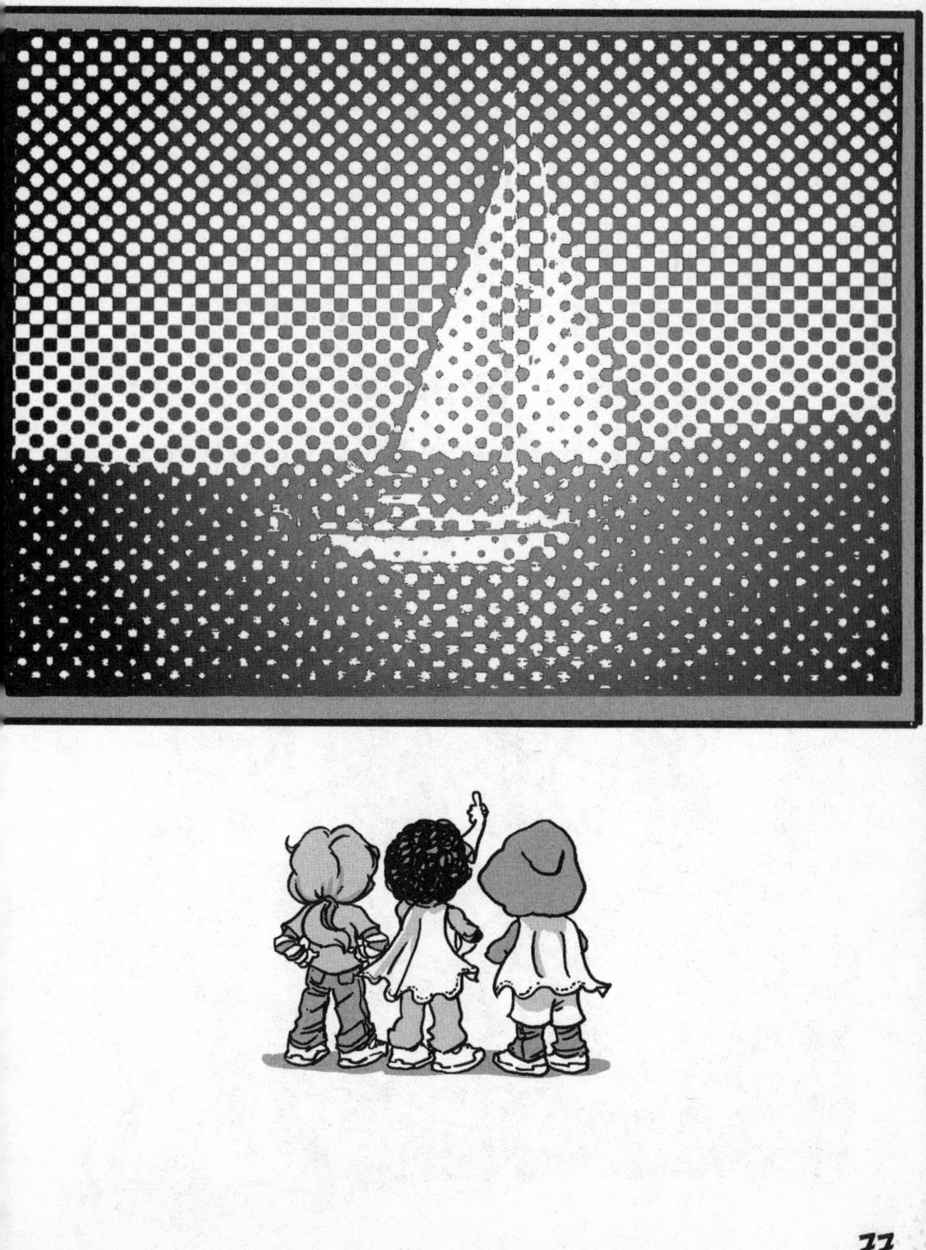

in code to hide the clue from bad guys looking for the treasure," said Supersonic Sal. "Good thing a superhero figured it out first!"

"My super brain tells me we should go to the right because that's the way the boat's facing," Captain Awesome suggested.

"HALT! Step away from the Sewer Rat!" The security guard from before stood at the far side of the room, pointing his flashlight at them.

"Will your evil ways never end?! It's pronounced 'Sir-ah!'" Captain Awesome called back.

"We can't let him get the treasure before we do!" Supersonic Sal grabbed Captain Awesome.

RUN!
DIVE!
HIDE!

The three heroes ran into the next room and dove behind the nearest display. They squished themselves down as low as they could and held their breath. The security guard stopped in front of them and scanned the room.

"I know you guys are in here!" he called. "Come on out!"

Trapped like the peas I hide under my mashed potatoes! Captain Awesome thought. *What would Super Dude do? Unleash his Super Dude Double Super Karate Chop? Or use his Super Dude Supertacular Heat Vision?*

But then Captain Awesome had a better idea.

He grabbed Nacho Cheese Man's can of cheese and threw it toward the door.

CLANG!
BANG!
CLATTER!
SPRAY!

The security guard spun toward the noise and raced from the room.

"Whew!" Captain Awesome sighed. "That was closer than the time Super Dude was almost tricked into eating Brussels Sproutonium by the Veggie Terrible!"

"But did you have to throw my can of cheese? That was a limited edition bacon and cheddar fla-vor." Nacho Cheese Man sighed.

"I'm sorry, chum," Captain

Awesome said in a heroic voice. "We all have to make some cheesy sacrifices in the battle against evil."

CHAPTER 8

Freeze!

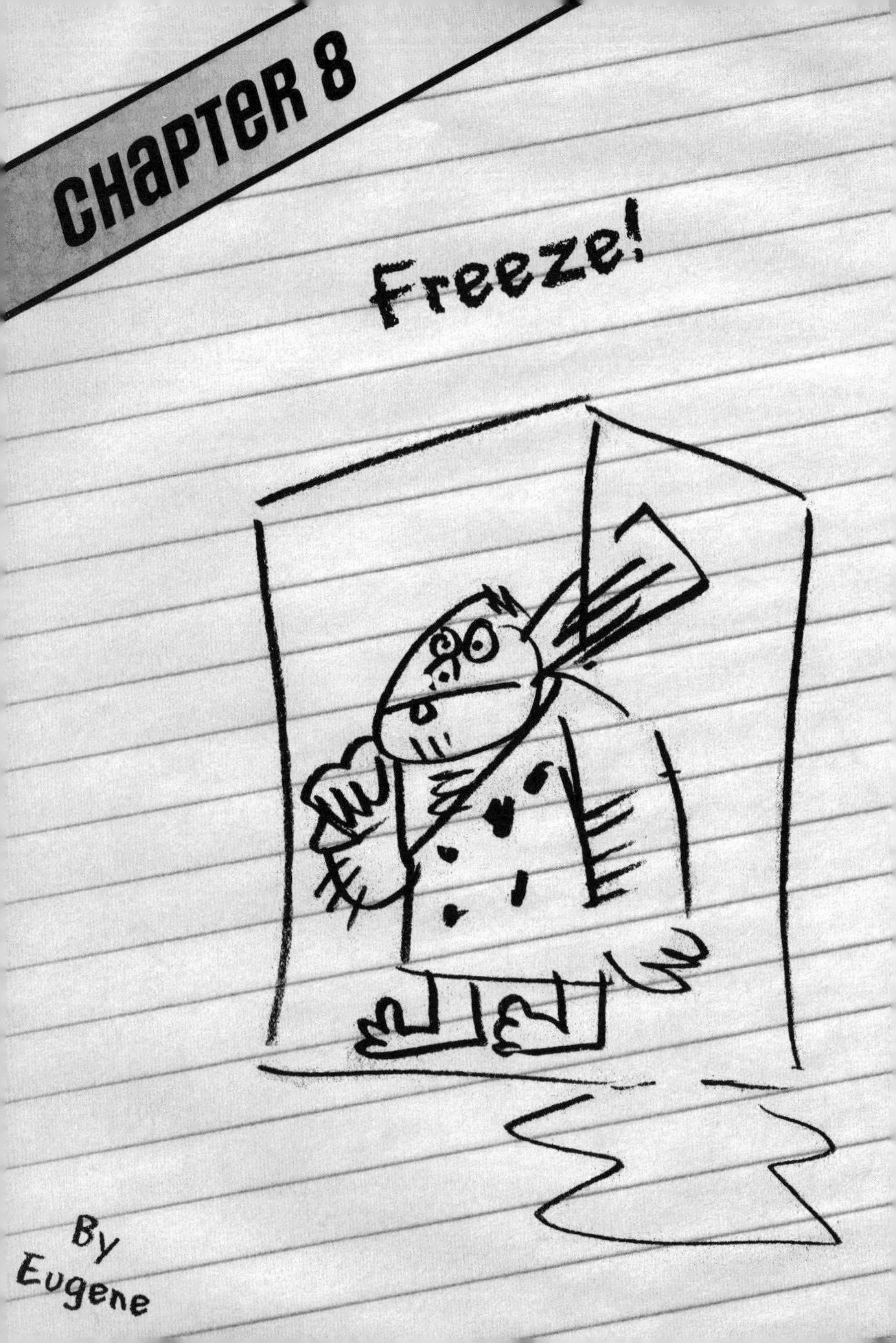

By Eugene

Captain Awesome peeked out from their hiding place. The guard was gone, but now he was face-to-face with the ugliest dude he had ever seen!

"Ahhh!" Captain Awesome yelled. He toppled into Nacho Cheese Man, who toppled into Supersonic Sal.

He was HAIRY!

He was UGLY!

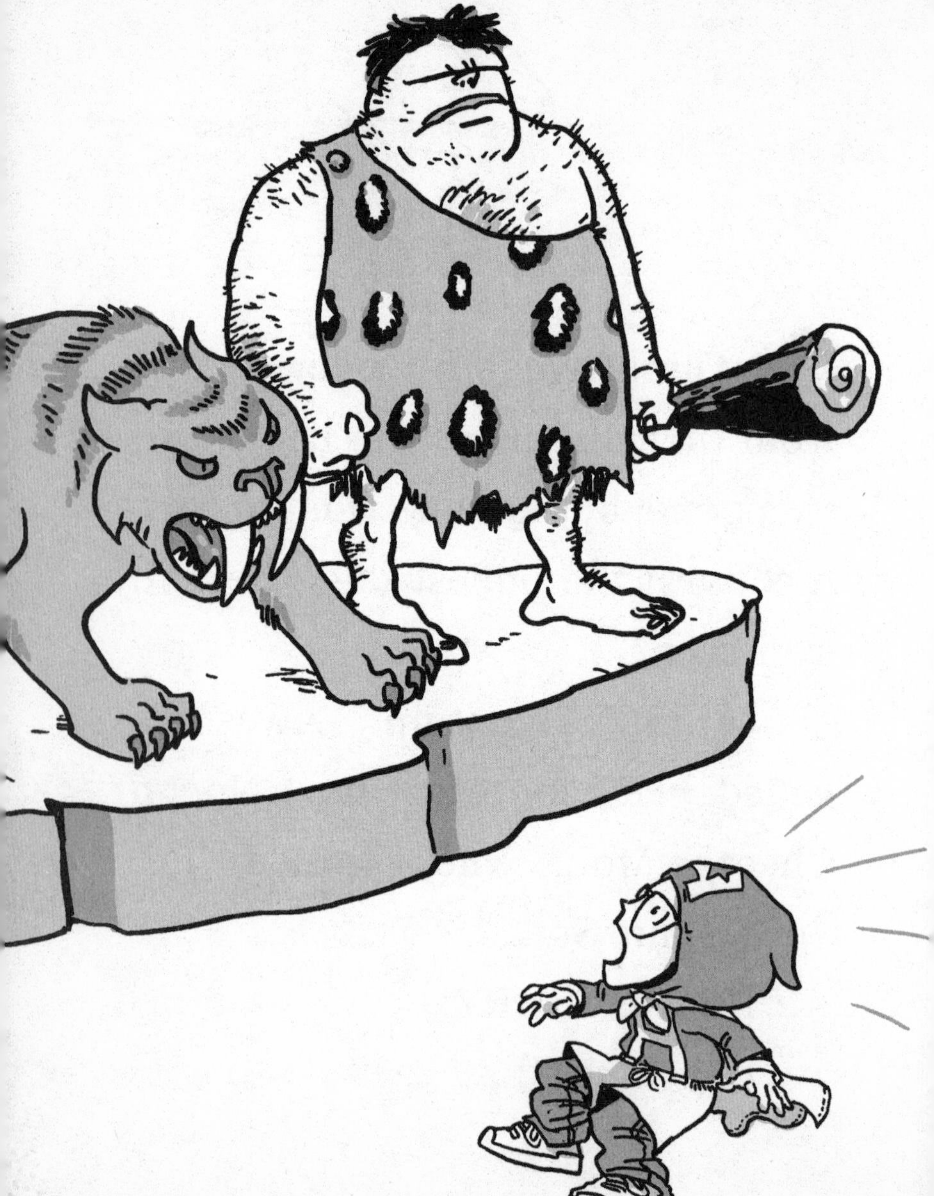

He was CAVEMAN-Y!

"S-sorry, sir! I didn't see you," Captain Awesome stammered.

But the hairy, ugly, caveman-y dude didn't answer. He just stood, club clenched in his hand, wearing an animal skin and looking hairy, ugly, and caveman-y.

"What's he staring at?" Nacho Cheese Man whispered.

"He's . . . he's not staring," Supersonic Sal realized. "He's *frozen!*"

And it wasn't just the caveman that was frozen. A saber-toothed tiger stood motionless next to him.

POKE! POKE!

The saber-toothed tiger didn't move.

POKE! POKE! POKE!

"I'll bet the security guard turned them into statues to stop them from finding the treasure," Supersonic Sal suggested.

POKE-POKE-POKE-POKE-
POKE-POKE-POKE-POKE!

"Why didn't I see it before?!"
Captain Awesome said as Nacho
Cheese Man continued poking
the saber-toothed tiger. "That's
no security guard! He's really the
fiendish Freeze Tagger and his Freeze
Light turned all these wild animals
into statues!"

"We've gotta find that treasure and get out of here before we're frozen too!" Nacho Cheese Man cried.

Supersonic Sal whipped out her notebook. "We need to find an eagle next!"

The superheroes scanned the room, their super senses focused like kids watching the clock tick off the final seconds of school. There were wooly mammoths, one with its trunk lifted high. Monkeys swung from fake trees and a polar bear stood

on a plastic
iceberg, but there was
no eagle.

"Well, looks
like the Freeze
Tagger turned all
these animals into
statues too," Captain
Awesome said.

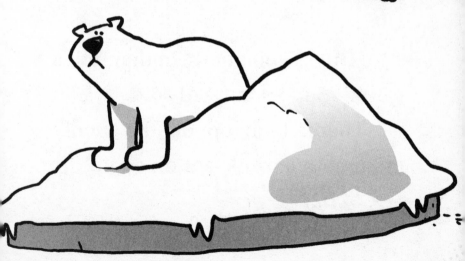

"Guys! Look at the mammoth's trunk!" Supersonic Sal said.

There, high up on the wooly mammoth's trunk, sat an eagle!
CLUE!

"We're on the right path!" Captain Awesome grinned. "What's the next clue?"

Before Supersonic Sal could reply, a light shone down on them. It was the Freeze Tagger with his Freeze Light!

"Finally! I found you guys!" the Freeze Tagger said. "Come with me."

"C-can't . . .
m-move . . . ,"
Nacho Cheese Man
stammered. "Legs
g-getting frozen by . . .
Freeze Light!"

"Fight it with
all your cheesy power!" Captain
Awesome yelled.

"Brain freezing
is worse than
drinking ten Super
Dude Super-Size
Slushies in an igloo!"
Supersonic Sal

tried to fight the
effects of
the Freeze
Tagger's
Freeze Light,
with no luck.

Must
muster all my superhero-ness in
one mighty superhero-y superchop!
Captain Awesome thought as he
willed his freezing arms to move.

SWING!
SMACK!
WHOOSH!

Captain Awesome spun and

knocked the Freeze Tagger's Freeze Light from his hand. It sailed across the room and landed on top of a wooly mammoth.

"You'll never turn us into statues, Freeze Tagger!"

Captain Awesome shouted as the three heroes ran from the room.

The security guard slumped

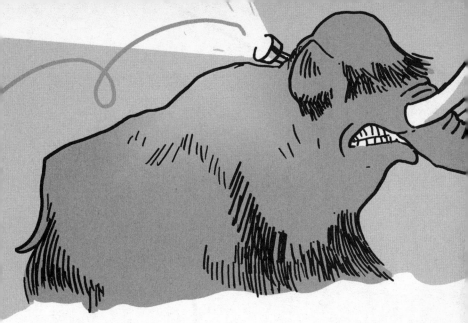

and rubbed his forehead with his hand. "I really hate when the museum has school field trips," he said aloud to no one.

CHAPTER 9

Treasure Room Triumph!

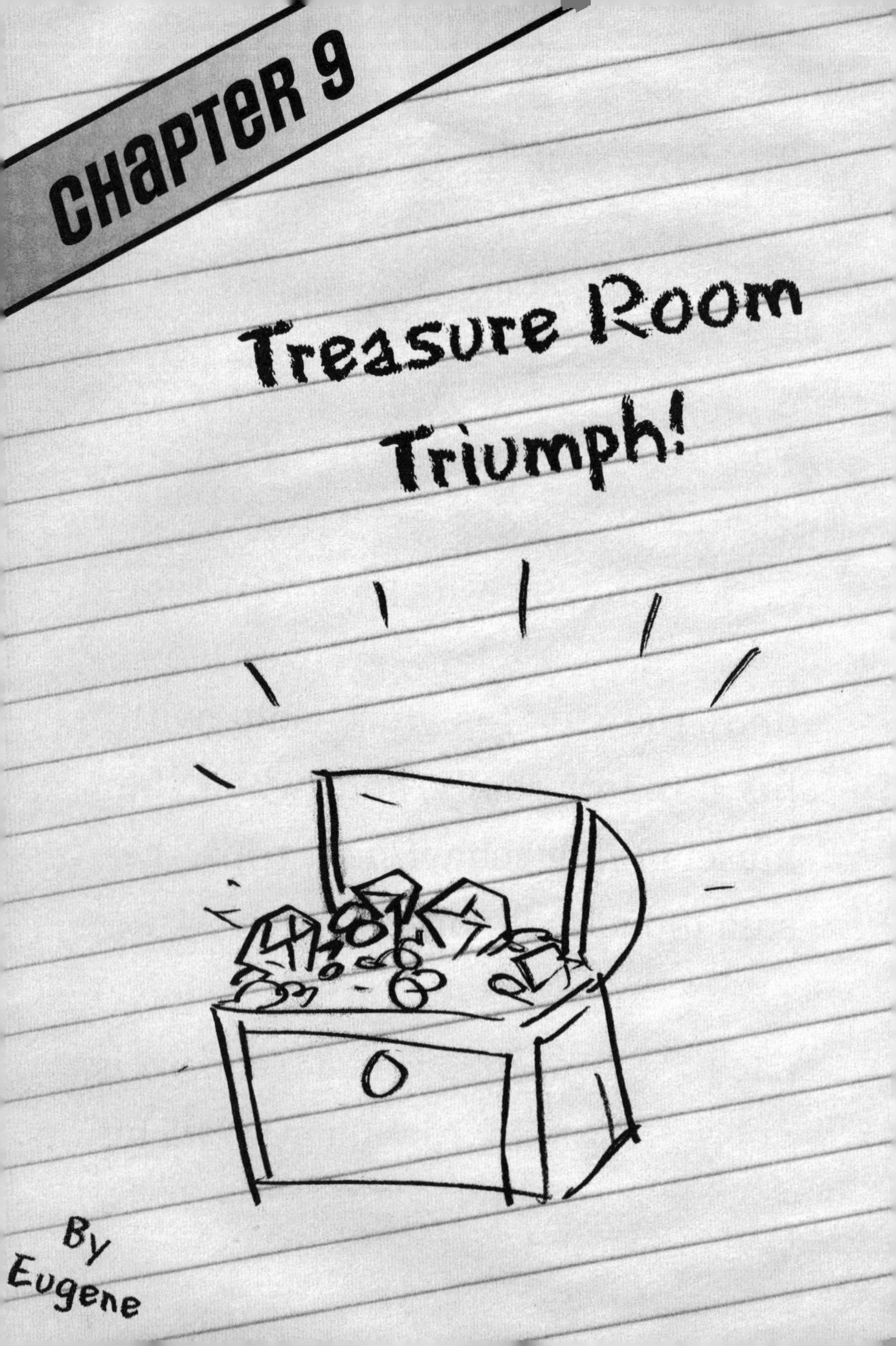

By Eugene

Captain Awesome, Supersonic Sal, and Nacho Cheese Man raced into the next room. Safe from the freeziness of the Freeze Tagger, Supersonic Sal whipped out her notebook to check for the next clue.

"Nothing," she said flipping to the last page. "The eagle was the final clue."

"So that means the treasure is here!" Captain Awesome used his

Awesome Vision Power to scan the room.

And that's when he saw it. . . .

Jewels the size of eggs and golden statues bigger than Super Dude. And Super Dude was one *big* dude!

"It's the mummy's treasure!" Nacho Cheese Man gasped, noticing the treasure too.

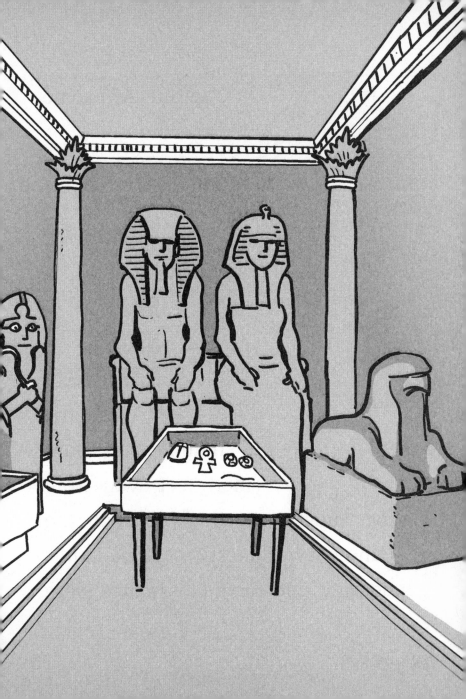

Captain Awesome led the charge!

"MI-TEEEEEE!"

"Wait!" Supersonic Sal called out.

SKID!
STOP!
TEACHERED!

With the mummy's treasure mere feet away from the superpowered fingers of the Sunnyview Superhero Squad, Ms. Beasley and their classmates were led into the room by Ms. Van Winkel.

RUN!

DIVE!

HIDE AGAIN!

"Welcome to the treasure room!"
the guide said.

The class *oooohed* and *aaaahed*.

"We've got to get the treasure before the Freeze Tagger finds us," Captain Awesome whispered.

"We *can't!*" Supersonic Sal whispered back. "We don't want to interrupt the tour, that'd just be rude."

"But the treasure's too treasureful to fall into the hands of bad guys," Captain Awesome whispered back.

The three heroes huddled.

WHISPER!

POINT! PLAN!

Captain Awesome, Nacho Cheese Man, and Supersonic Sal broke away from the huddle. They gave a silent three-way Sunnyview Super Squad Super Mission Salute before they quietly scattered around the room and awaited the signal.

CHAPTER 10

Misguided by the Miss Leader

By
Eugene

Captain Awesome slooowly raised his hand, ready to give the signal.

Supersonic Sal nervously bit her fingers.

Nacho Cheese Man reached for his can of cheese . . . but then remembered it was gone.

Come on . . . almost ready . . . Captain Awesome thought. *Three . . . two . . . one . . .*

But just
as Captain
Awesome
was about
to leap from
his hiding place,
the Freeze Tag-
ger marched into the
room, his Freeze Light
clenched in his hand.

"They ran off
again. I'm not sure where they
went," the Freeze Tagger said to
Ms. Van Winkel.

SHOCK!

GASP!
DOUBLE SHOCK!

Captain Awesome realized the truth. *That's no normal tour guide! She must be the Miss Leader, the evil villain who misleads kids on field trips so they never get out of museums without being bored to sleep!*

"That's it! Sunnyview Superhero Squad CHAAAARRRRRRRGE!" Captain Awesome called out.

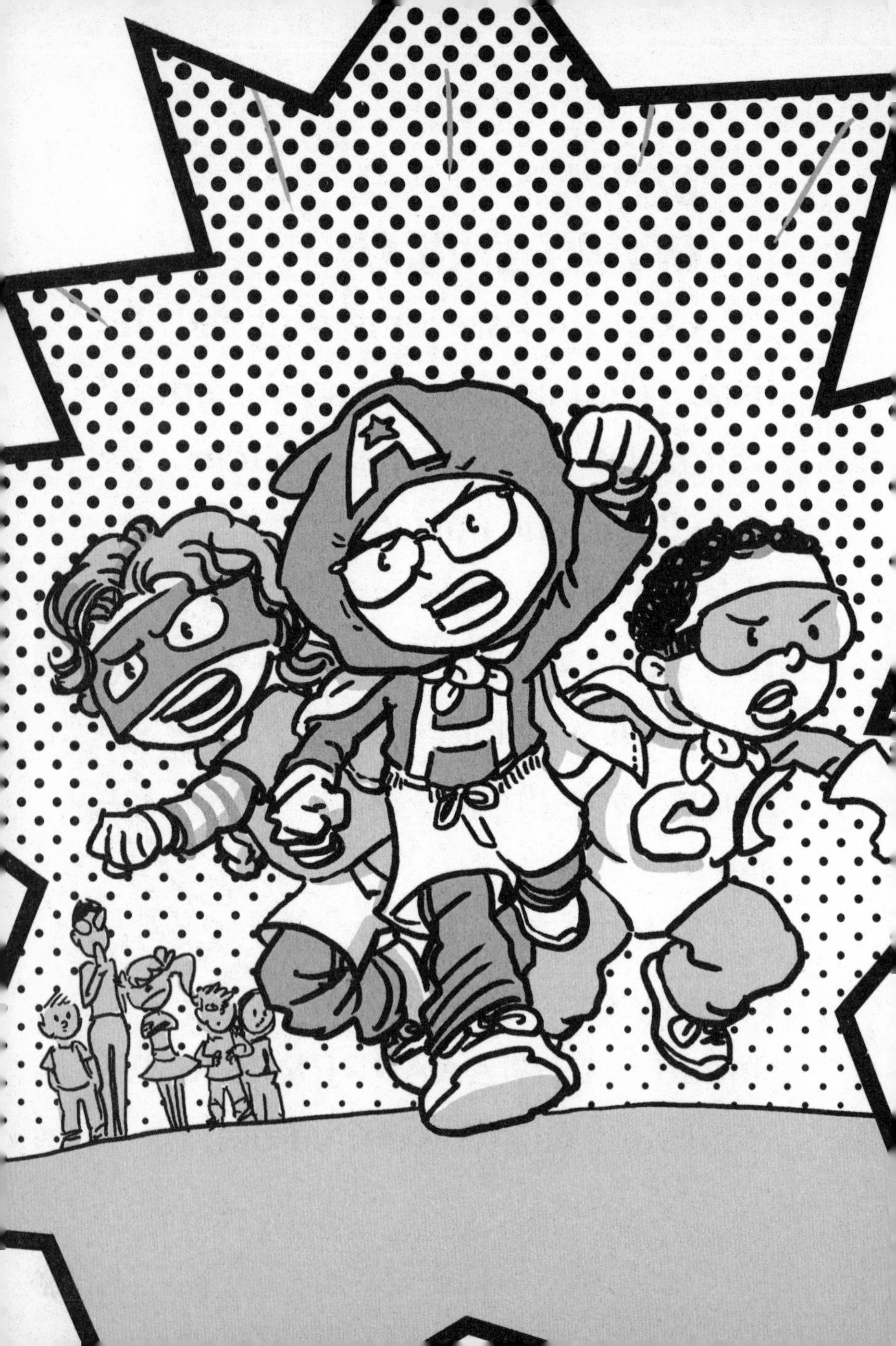

In a flash Supersonic Sal, Nacho Cheese Man, and Captain Awesome raced from their hiding places and ran straight for the treasure.

"Hands off that treasure, super-villains!" Captain Awesome called out. "We'll never let you take it!"

"Here we go again," Meredith groaned. "Can't we leave them on the bus next time?"

"Eugene—I mean, uh, Captain Awesome—I know I'm going to regret asking, but what's going on?" Ms. Beasley asked.

"That's Freeze Tagger and the Miss Leader! They're here to steal the mummy's treasure!" Captain Awesome thrust an accusing finger at the security guard and the tour guide.

"*Steal* the treasure?" a shocked Ms. Van Winkel asked. "We'd never do that! We *guard* the treasure and make sure everyone can see it.

That's what makes museums so *special*. They share the world's treasures for everyone to enjoy."

"Then why was the Freeze Tagger—I mean the security guy—after us?" Captain Awesome asked.

"I thought you were lost and I wanted to help you get back to your class," the security guard explained.

"Sounds like this was all one big misunderstanding," Ms. Beasley said.

"Not the first time." Meredith sneered and crossed her arms.

"Now why don't you three rejoin our tour?" the tour guide asked. "I was about to tell everyone the amazing history of the treasure and the pharaoh who buried it. . . ."

"That would be MI-TEE!" Captain Awesome cheered. Although he, Nacho Cheese Man, and Supersonic Sal were pretty sure they already knew *that* story.

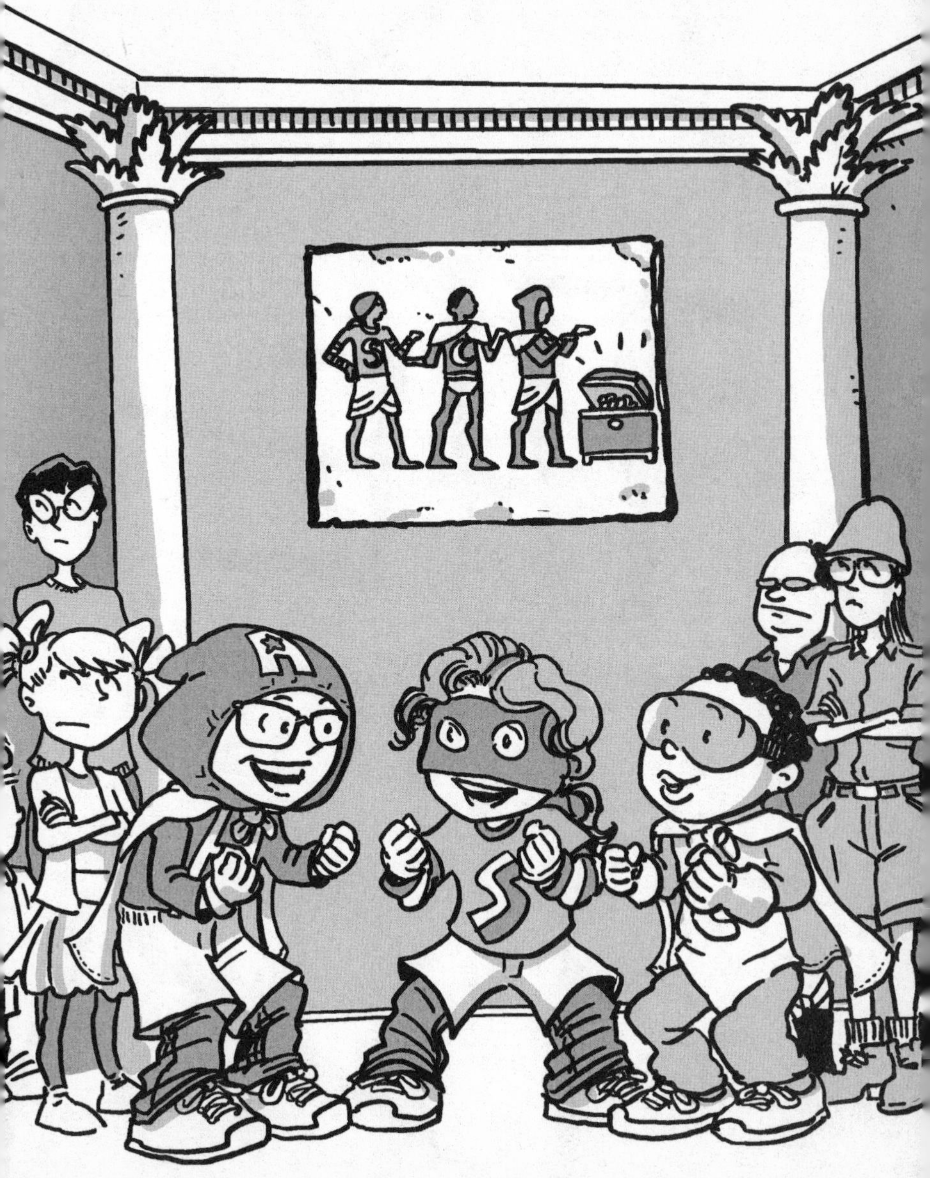

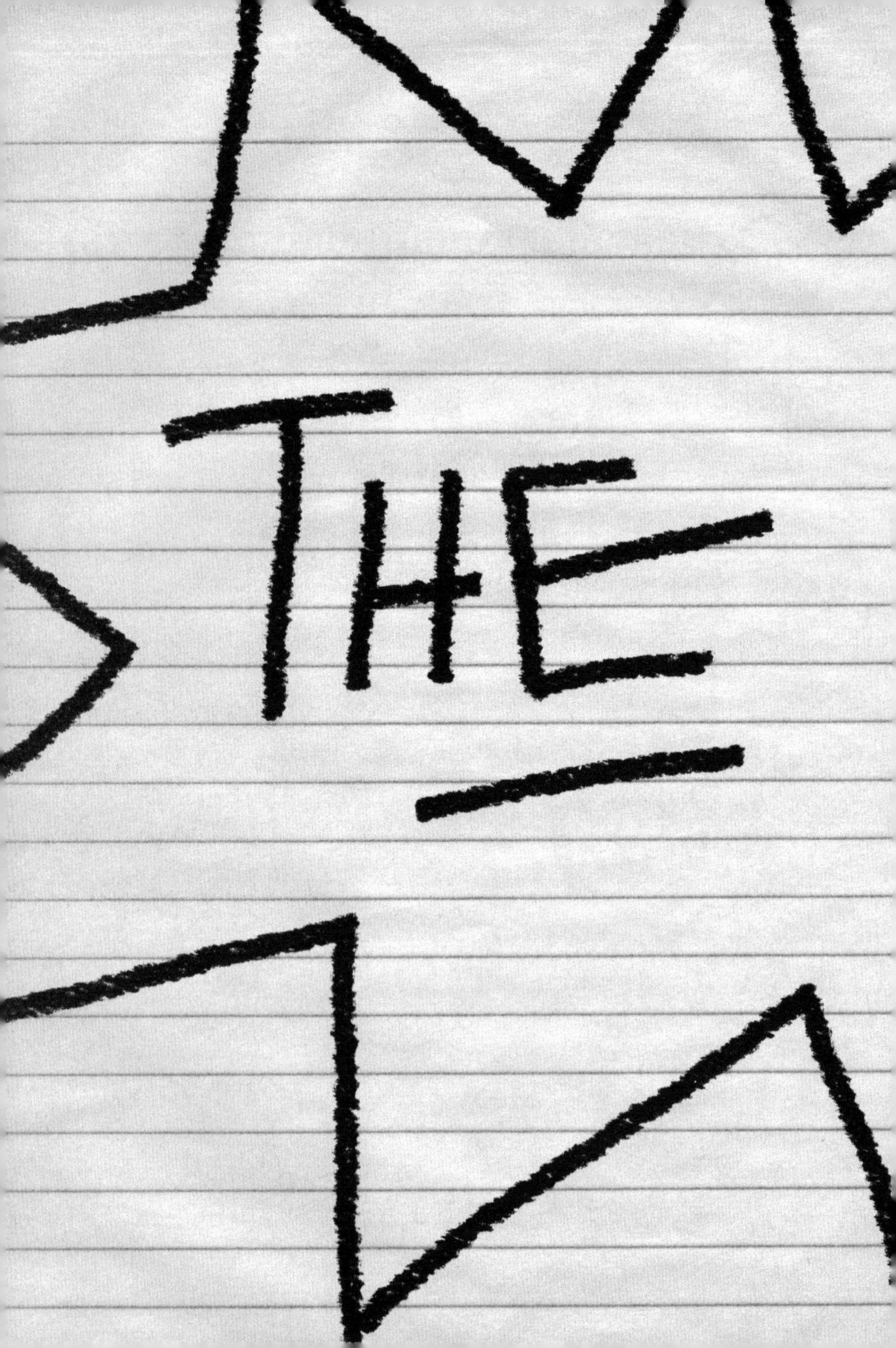
THE

END!

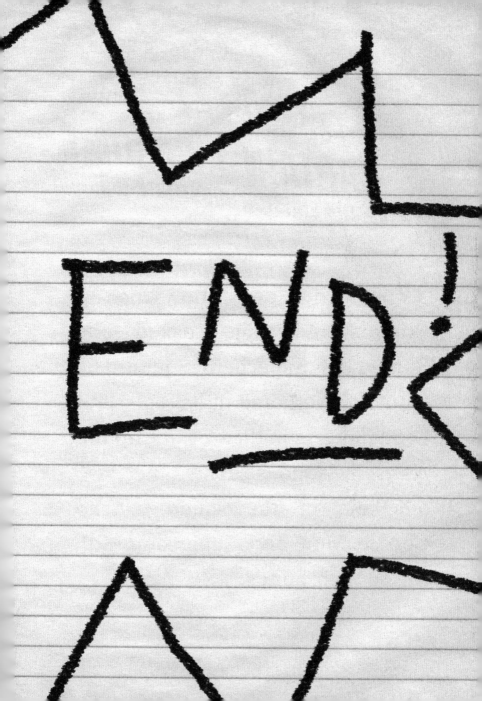

Keep reading for a sneak peek at the next Captain Awesome adventure!

CAPTAIN AWESOME
VS. THE SINISTER SUBSTITUTE TEACHER

Worst day of the week?" Captain Awesome asked the Sunnyview Superhero Squad. The team had gathered at its top-secret headquarters in the tree at Captain Awesome's house. The other two members of the squad, Nacho Cheese Man and Supersonic Sal, raised their hands.

Nacho Cheese Man said, "Any day I run out of spray cheese and have to fight evil the old fashioned way. With American Cheese slices."

But Captain Awesome knew what the real worst day was. "It's Sunday," he said. "It's the last day of the weekend, and our crime-fighting stops since we have to go to school."

"But crime-fighting never stops," Supersonic Sal pointed out.

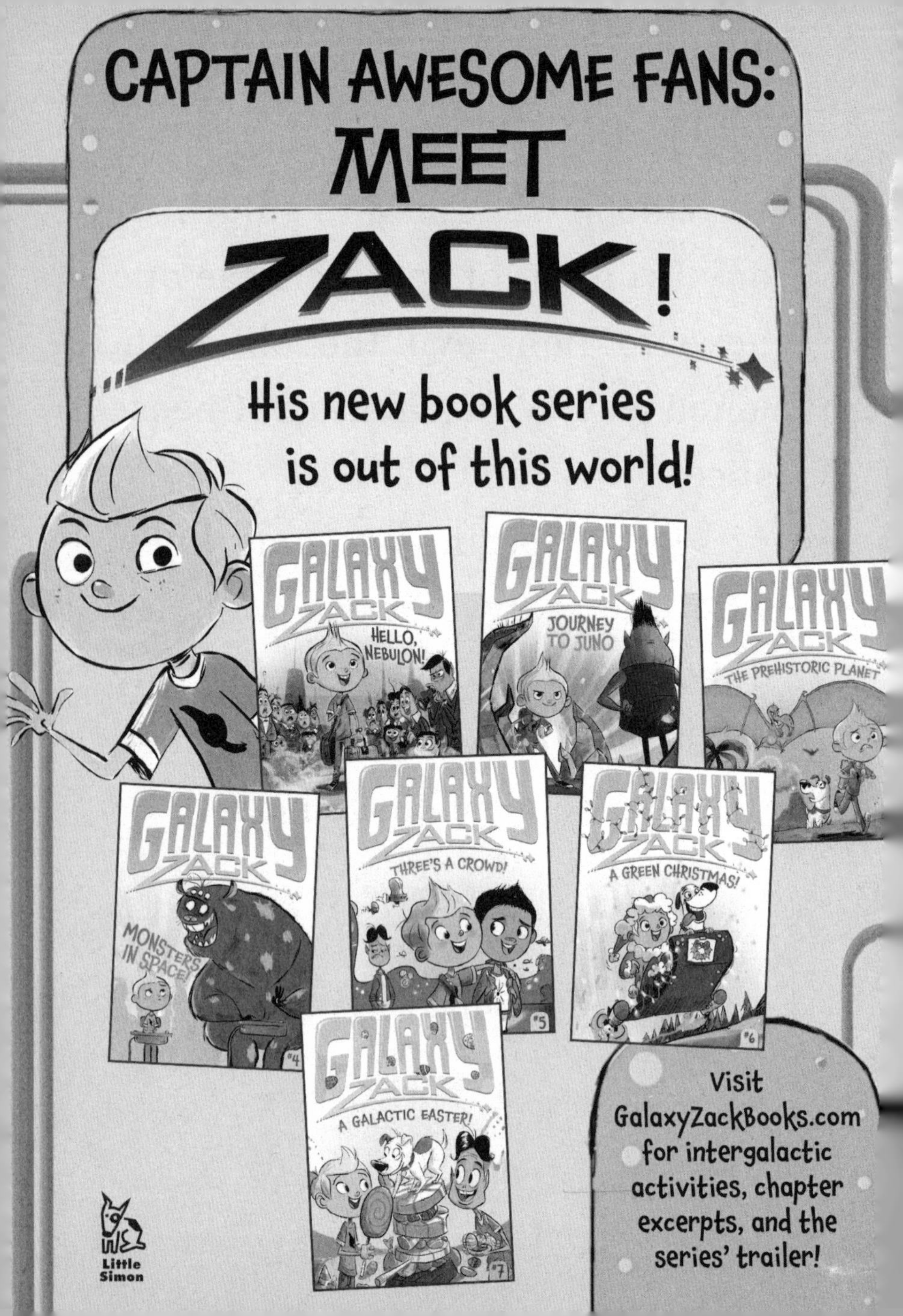

CAPTAIN AWESOME FANS:
MEET
ZACK!
His new book series is out of this world!
GALAXY ZACK
HELLO, NEBULON!
GALAXY ZACK
JOURNEY TO JUNO
GALAXY ZACK
THE PREHISTORIC PLANET
GALAXY ZACK
MONSTERS IN SPACE!
#4
GALAXY ZACK
THREE'S A CROWD!
#5
GALAXY ZACK
A GREEN CHRISTMAS!
#6
GALAXY ZACK
A GALACTIC EASTER!
#7
Visit GalaxyZackBooks.com for intergalactic activities, chapter excerpts, and the series' trailer!
Little Simon